WALTZING MATILDA

Angus&Robertson
An imprint of HarperCollins*Publishers,* Australia

First published in Australia by William Collins Pty Ltd in 1970
First published in paperback in 1979
Reprinted in 1981, 1982, 1984 (twice), 1985, 1986, 1987 (twice), 1989
This edition published in 1990,
Reprinted in 1992, 1994, 1996
by HarperCollins*Publishers* Pty Limited
ACN 009 913 517
A member of the HarperCollins*Publishers* (Australia) Pty Limited Group

Copyright © This edition HarperCollinsPublishers 1992
Illustrations: Desmond Digby 1970

HarperCollins*Publishers*
25 Ryde Road, Pymble, Sydney, NSW 2073, Australia
31 View Road, Glenfield, Auckland 10, New Zealand
77-85 Fulham Palace Road, London W6 8JB, United Kingdom
Hazelton Lanes, 55 Avenue Road, Suite 2900, Toronto, Ontario M5R 3L2
and 1995 Markham Road, Scarborough, Ontario M1B 5M8, Canada
10 East 53rd Street, New York NY 10032, USA

National Library of Australia Cataloguing-in-Publication data:

Paterson, A. B. (Andrew Barton), 1864–1941.
  Waltzing matlda.
  ISBN 0 207 17098 3.
  1. Children's poetry, Australia.
  I. Digby, Desmond, 1933–   . II. Title.
A821'.2

Typeset by Computype, Sydney
Printed in Australia by Cranbrook Colour

17 16 15 14
99 98 97 96

To Marjorie Cotton.
Ɗ.W.Ɗ.

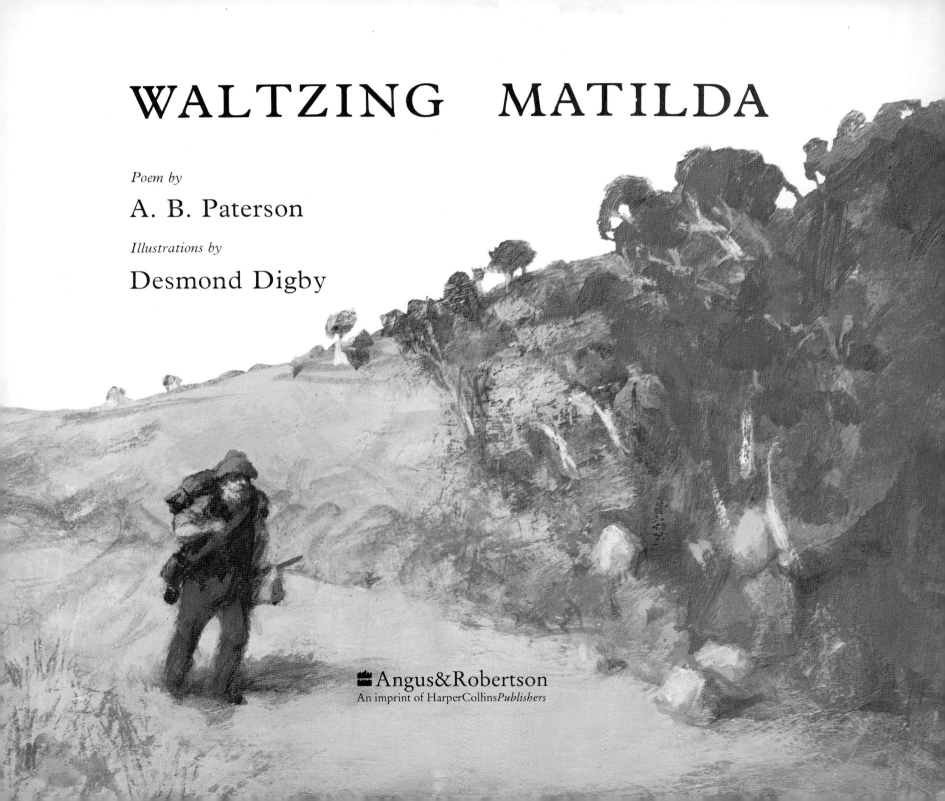

WALTZING MATILDA

Poem by

A. B. Paterson

Illustrations by

Desmond Digby

Angus&Robertson
An imprint of HarperCollins*Publishers*

Oh! There once was a swagman camped in a Billabong,

Under the shade of a Coolabah tree;

And he sang as he looked at his old billy boiling,

"Who'll come a-waltzing Matilda with me?"

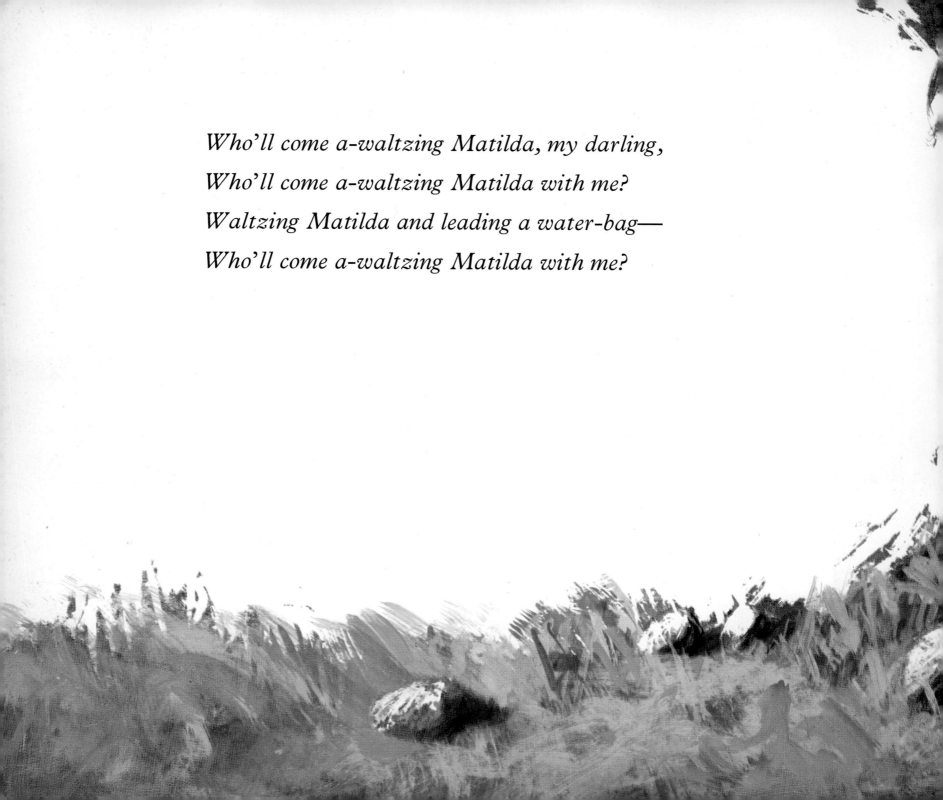

Who'll come a-waltzing Matilda, my darling,
Who'll come a-waltzing Matilda with me?
Waltzing Matilda and leading a water-bag—
Who'll come a-waltzing Matilda with me?

Down came a jumbuck to drink at the water-hole,

Up jumped the swagman and grabbed him in glee;

And he sang as he stowed him away in his tucker-bag,

"You'll come a-waltzing Matilda with me!"

Who'll come a-waltzing Matilda, my darling,
Who'll come a-waltzing Matilda with me?
Waltzing Matilda and leading a water-bag—
Who'll come a-waltzing Matilda with me?

Down came the Squatter a-riding his thoroughbred;

Down came Policemen—one,

two

and three.

"Whose is the jumbuck you've got in your tucker-bag?

You'll come a-waltzing Matilda with me."

Who'll come a-waltzing Matilda, my darling,
Who'll come a-waltzing Matilda with me?
Waltzing Matilda and leading a water-bag—
Who'll come a-waltzing Matilda with me?

But the swagman, he up and he jumped in the water-hole,

Drowning himself by the Coolabah tree;

And his ghost may be heard as it sings in the billabong,

"Who'll come a-waltzing Matilda with me?"

GLOSSARY

BILLABONG: A backwater from an inland river, sometimes returning to it and sometimes ending in sand.
Except in flood times it is usually a dried-up channel
containing a series of pools or waterholes.

BILLY: A cylindrical tin pot with a lid and a wire handle
used as a bushman's kettle.

COOLABAH TREE: A species of Eucalyptus, *E. microtheca,*
common in the Australian inland where it grows
along watercourses.

JUMBUCK: A sheep. From an Aboriginal word, the original
meaning of which is obscure.

SQUATTER: Originally applied to a person who placed
himself on public land without a licence, it was ex-
tended to describe a pastoralist who rented large tracts
of Crown land for grazing and later to one who held
his sheep run as freehold.

SWAGMAN: A man who, carrying his personal possessions
in a bundle or SWAG, travels on foot in the country in
search of casual or seasonal employment. A tramp.

WALTZING MATILDA: Carrying a swag; possibly a cor-
ruption of 'walking matilda'. 'Matilda' was a type of
swag where the clothes and personal belongings were
wrapped in a long blanket roll and tied towards each
end like a Christmas cracker. It was carried around
the neck with the loose ends falling down each side in
front, one end clasped by the arm.